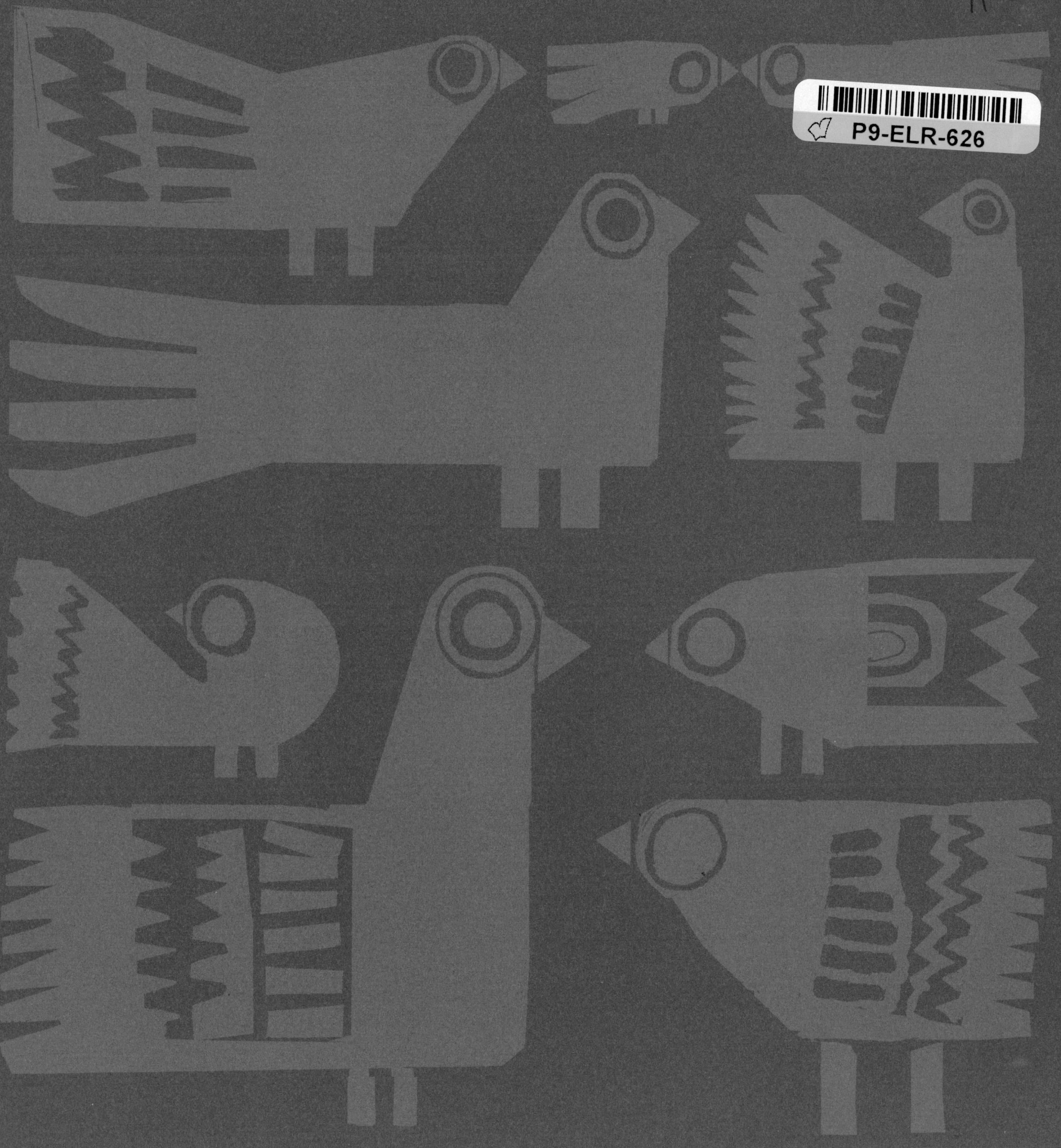

Shh!
WE HAVE A PLAN

CHRIS HAUGHTON

CANDLEWICK PRESS

Peace cannot be kept
by force. It can only be
achieved by understanding.

Albert Einstein

To my youngest sister, Lynn

First U.S. edition 2014

Library of Congress Catalog Card Number 2013955701

ISBN 978-0-7636-7293-5

TLF 19 18
14 13 12 11

Printed in Dongguan, Guangdong, China

This book was typeset in SHH.
The illustrations were created digitally.

Candlewick Press
99 Dover Street
Somerville, Massachusetts 02144

visit us at www.candlewick.com

FSC
www.fsc.org

MIX
Paper from
responsible sources
FSC® C104723

Shh!
WE HAVE A PLAN
CHRIS HAUGHTON

hello,
birdie

shh   SHH!   we have a plan.

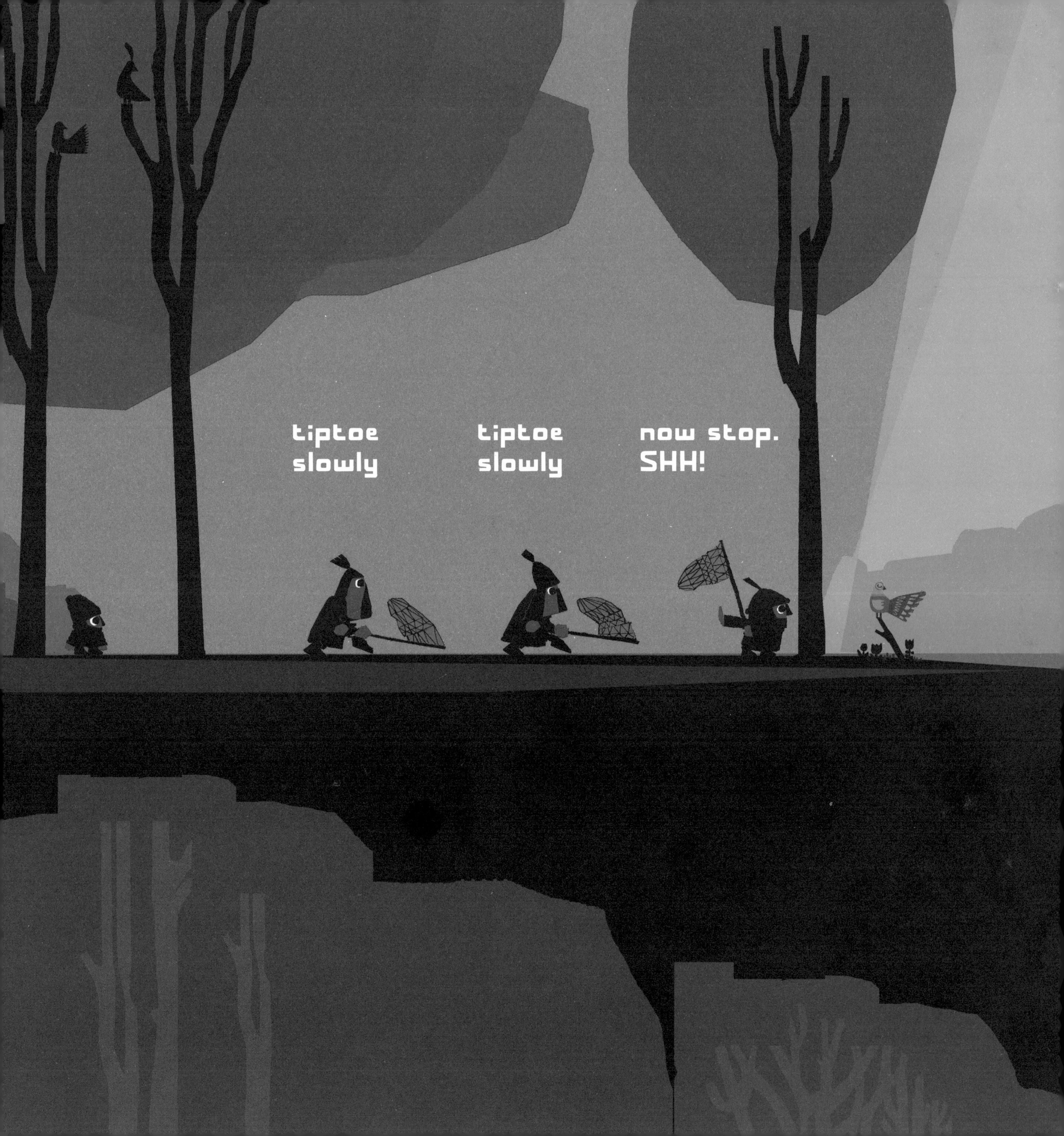

tiptoe
slowly

tiptoe
slowly

now stop.
SHH!

ready one

ready two   ready three . . .

LOOK!
up there

hello,
birdie

shh   SHH!   we have a plan.

ready
one

ready
two

ready
three . . .

LOOK!
down there

hello,
birdie

shh   SHH!   we have a plan.

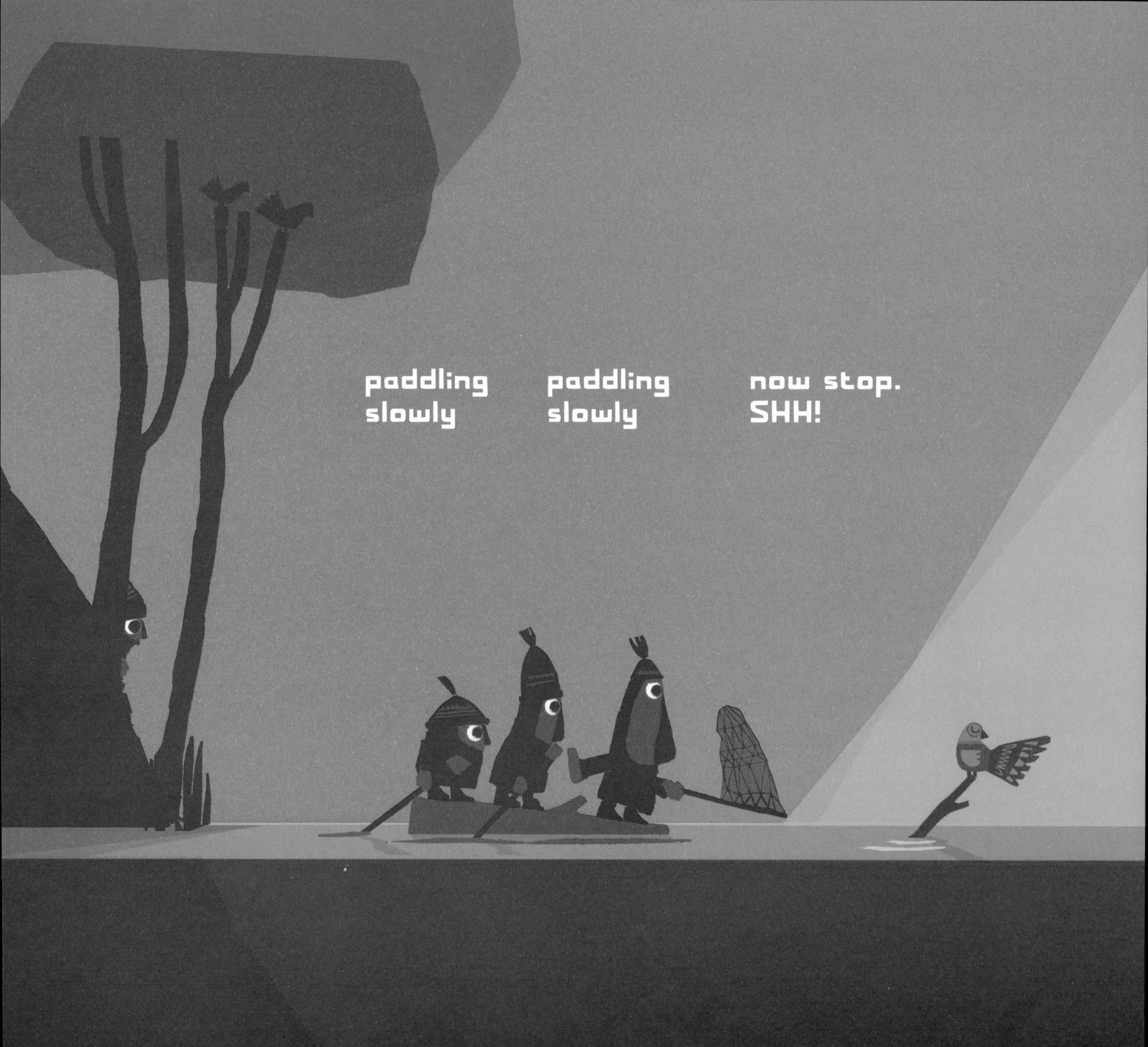

paddling
slowly

paddling
slowly

now stop.
SHH!

ready
one

ready
two

ready
three . . .

hello, birdie

would you like
some bread?

one

two

three

LOOK!

ready th . . .

RUN AWAY!

SHH! we have a plan.

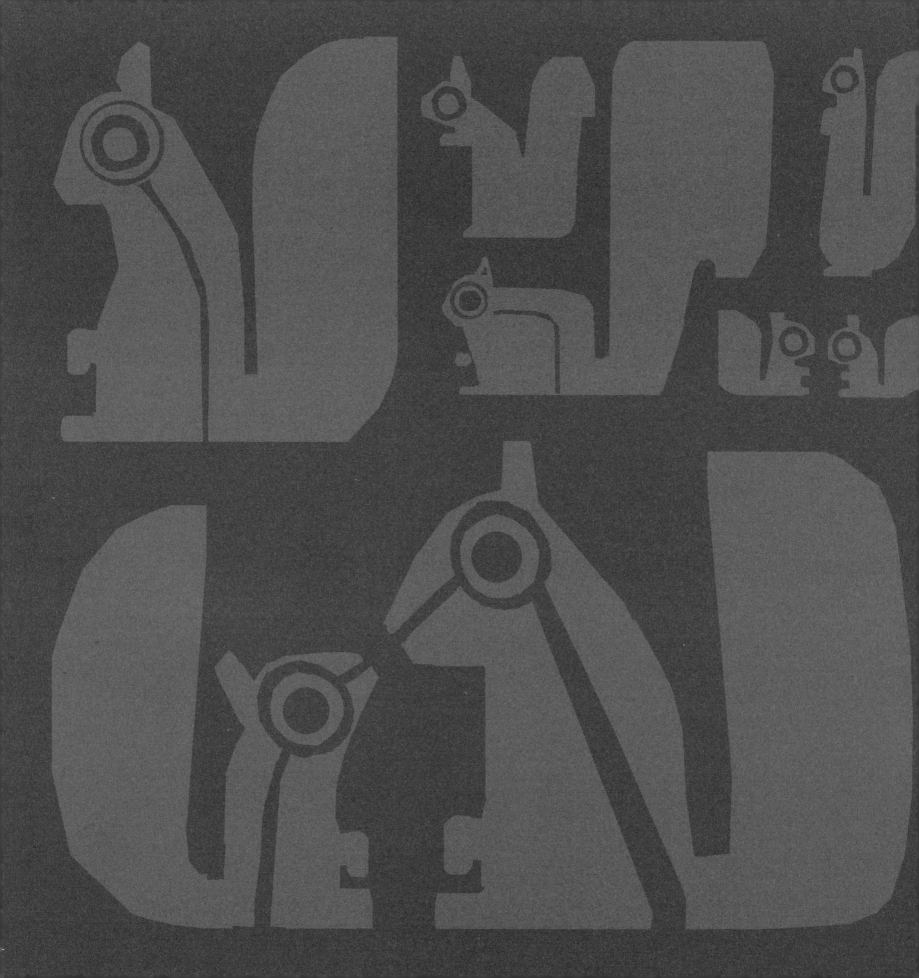